THE BIG

MILLY-
MOLLY-
MANDY

STORYBOOK

It's good to be sitting still,
And it's good to be running wild,
And it's good to be by yourself alone
Or with another child.

And whether the child's grown up,
Or whether the child is small,
So long as it really is a Child
It doesn't matter at all.

J.L.B.

For my Mum and Dad –
with love, C.V.

Publisher's Note

The stories in this collection are reproduced in the form in which they appeared
upon first publication in the UK by George G. Harrap & Co. Ltd.
All spellings remain consistent with these original editions.

KINGFISHER
An imprint of Kingfisher Publications Plc
New Penderel House, 283-288 High Holborn, London WC1V 7HZ
Larousse Kingfisher Chambers Inc.
95 Madison Avenue, New York, New York 10016

First published by Kingfisher 2000
2 4 6 8 10 9 7 5 3 1
1TR/0600/TWP/FR/150SIN

Many of these stories first appeared in the Children's Page of the
Christian Science Monitor (beginning with "Milly-Molly-Mandy Goes Errands" in 1925).
They first appeared in book form in
Milly-Molly-Mandy Stories (1928)
More of Milly-Molly-Mandy (1929)
Further Doings of Milly-Molly-Mandy (1932)
Milly-Molly-Mandy Again (1948)
Milly-Molly-Mandy & Co (1955)
published by George G. Harrap & Co. Ltd.

A CIP catalogue record for this book is available from the British Library.
LIBRARY OF CONGRESS CATALOGING IN PUBLICATION DATA
has been applied for.

ISBN 0 7534 0483 4 (UK)
ISBN 0 7534 5331 2 (US)

Printed in Singapore

THE BIG
MILLY-
MOLLY-
MANDY
STORYBOOK

JOYCE LANKESTER BRISLEY

With new illustrations by

CLARA VULLIAMY

KINGFISHER

Contents

Grandpa   Grandma   Uncle   Aunty

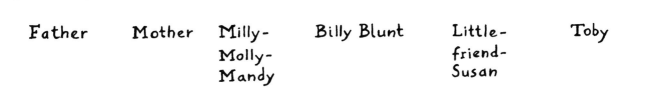

Father   Mother   Milly-   Billy Blunt   Little-   Toby
Molly-   friend-
Mandy   Susan

Foreword

NOTHING EVOKES THE HAPPINESS OF CHILDHOOD so vividly as rediscovering a treasured storybook, and for me none more so than the Milly-Molly-Mandy stories. As a child I would read and re-read and savour every detail with my mother who had so enjoyed them herself when she was young. Milly-Molly-Mandy was so real to me that if she'd come running up the garden path with Toby the dog at her heels I shouldn't have been a bit surprised! And now I'm sharing her adventures with my own children.

What a delight, then, to have the chance to illustrate these stories myself, seventy-five years after their first appearance. It involved no effort of will to be true to Joyce Lankester Brisley's original black-and-white drawings, for her words could not be pictured in any other way. Her visual interpretation of her characters and the world they inhabit is an integral part of the stories, most especially with Milly-Molly-Mandy herself: her fresh, happy face alive with irrepressible optimism, her plump little legs, her untidy bob, her bright button eyes – she *is* how she looks.

Somehow, magically, Joyce Lankester Brisley's black-and-white illustration suggests its own colour – I just knew that Milly-Molly-Mandy was pink-cheeked with excitement (and pink-kneed with the cold) with hair the colour of the darkest part of a conker, and that by contrast little-friend-Susan, with her golden curls, was an English rose in powder blue. So to recreate in colour was pure pleasure – to paint the cottage gardens, the hedgerows changing with the seasons, the seaside, but the children best of all.

Reading these stories to my children today, so long after they were written, I'm struck by how much is recognizable and familiar to them, though of course there is plenty that is different. One glance at the map of the village – which Milly-Molly-Mandy so rarely leaves – tells us that her world is small: living in the nice white cottage with her extended family, where the neighbours all know each other; playing out of doors with her friends, inventing their own fun, safe and free. Mother and Milly-Molly-Mandy each have their separate roles to play. Mother is definitely not the type to sit on the floor and play with Milly-Molly-Mandy and a tipped-out toy box – more likely instead to give her a handful of raisins and a little task to do ("My Muvver says we'd be like apple-trees which didn't grow apples if we didn't be useful.").

The children's days are full of adventure and incident. And more telling still are the many ways the children find to fill the time while waiting for the big event – the snow, the party, the day at the sea . . . timeless, beautifully observed and described with charm, humour and subtlety. They remind us that, despite everything, children haven't changed a bit.

May 2000

Milly-Molly-Mandy Goes Errands

ONCE UPON A TIME there was a little girl.

She had a Father, and a Mother, and a Grandpa, and a Grandma, and an Uncle, and an Aunty; and they all lived together in a nice white cottage with a thatched roof.

This little girl had short hair, and short legs, and short frocks (pink-and-white-striped cotton in summer, and red serge in winter). But her name wasn't short at all. It was Millicent Margaret Amanda. But Father and Mother and Grandpa and Grandma and Uncle and Aunty couldn't very well call out "Millicent Margaret Amanda!" every time they wanted her, so they shortened it to "Milly-Molly-Mandy," which is quite easy to say.

Now everybody in the nice white cottage with the thatched roof had some particular job to do – even Milly-Molly-Mandy.

Father grew vegetables in the big garden by the cottage. Mother cooked the dinners and did the washing. Grandpa took the vegetables to market in his little pony-cart. Grandma knitted socks and mittens and nice warm woollies for them all. Uncle kept cows (to give them milk) and chickens (to give them eggs). Aunty sewed frocks and shirts for them, and did the sweeping and dusting.

And Milly-Molly-Mandy, what did she do?

Well, Milly-Molly-Mandy's legs were short, as I've told you, but they were very lively, just right for running errands. So Milly-Molly-Mandy was quite busy, fetching and carrying things, and taking messages.

One fine day Milly-Molly-Mandy was in the garden playing with Toby the dog, when Father poked his head out from the other side of a big row of beans, and said:

"Milly-Molly-Mandy, run down to Mr Moggs' cottage and ask for the trowel he borrowed from me!"

So Milly-Molly-Mandy said, "Yes, Farver!" and ran in to get her hat.

At the kitchen door was Mother, with a basket of eggs in her hand. And when she saw Milly-Molly-Mandy she said:

"Milly-Molly-Mandy, run down to Mrs Moggs and give her these eggs. She's got visitors."

So Milly-Molly-Mandy said, "Yes, Muvver!" and took the basket. "Trowel for Farver, eggs for Muvver," she thought to herself.

Then Grandpa came up and said:

"Milly-Molly-Mandy, please get me a ball of string from Miss Muggins' shop – here's the penny."

So Milly-Molly-Mandy said, "Yes, Grandpa!" and took the penny, thinking to herself, "Trowel for Farver, eggs for Muvver, string for Grandpa."

As she passed through the kitchen Grandma, who was sitting in her armchair knitting, said:

"Milly-Molly-Mandy, will you get me a skein of red wool? Here's a sixpence."

So Milly-Molly-Mandy said, "Yes, Grandma!" and took the sixpence. "Trowel for Farver, eggs for Muvver, string for Grandpa, red wool for Grandma," she whispered over to herself.

As she went into the passage Uncle came striding up in a hurry.

"Oh, Milly-Molly-Mandy," said Uncle, "run like a good girl to Mr Blunt's shop, and tell him I'm waiting for the chicken-feed he promised to send!"

So Milly-Molly-Mandy said, "Yes, Uncle!" and thought to herself, "Trowel for Farver, eggs for Muvver, string for Grandpa, red wool for Grandma, chicken-feed for Uncle."

As she got her hat off the peg Aunty called from the parlour where she was dusting:

"Is that Milly-Molly-Mandy? Will you get me a packet of needles, dear? Here's a penny!"

So Milly-Molly-Mandy said, "Yes, Aunty!" and took the penny, thinking to herself, "Trowel for Farver, eggs for Muvver, string for Grandpa, red wool for Grandma, chicken-feed for Uncle, needles for Aunty, and I do hope there won't be anything more!"

But there was nothing else, so Milly-Molly-Mandy started out down the path. When she came to the gate Toby the dog capered up, looking very excited at the thought of a walk. But Milly-Molly-Mandy eyed him solemnly, and said:

"Trowel for Farver, eggs for Muvver, string for Grandpa, red wool for Grandma, chicken-feed for Uncle, needles for Aunty. No, Toby, you mustn't come now, I've too much to think about. But I promise to take you for a walk when I come back!"

So she left Toby on the other side of the gate, and set off down the road, with the basket and the pennies and the sixpence.

Presently she met a little friend, and the little friend said:

"Hullo, Milly-Molly-Mandy! I've got a new see-saw! Do come on it with me!"

But Milly-Molly-Mandy looked at her solemnly and said:

"Trowel for Farver, eggs for Muvver, string for Grandpa, red wool for Grandma, chicken-feed for Uncle, needles for Aunty. No, Susan, I can't come now, I'm busy. But I'd like to come when I get back – after I've taken Toby for a walk."

So Milly-Molly-Mandy went on her way with the basket and the pennies and the sixpence.

Soon she came to the Moggs' cottage.

"Please, Mrs Moggs, can I have the trowel for Farver? And here are some eggs from Muvver!" she said.

Mrs Moggs was very much obliged indeed for the eggs, and fetched the trowel and a piece of seed-cake for Milly-Molly-Mandy's own self. And Milly-Molly-Mandy went on her way with the empty basket.

Next she came to Miss Muggins' little shop.

"Please, Miss Muggins, can I have a ball of string for Grandpa and a skein of red wool for Grandma?"

So Miss Muggins put the string and the wool into Milly-Molly-Mandy's basket, and took a penny and a sixpence in exchange. So that left Milly-Molly-Mandy with one penny. And Milly-Molly-Mandy couldn't remember what that penny was for.

"Sweeties, perhaps?" said Miss Muggins, glancing at the row of glass bottles on the shelf.

But Milly-Molly-Mandy shook her head.

"No," she said, "and it can't be chicken-feed for Uncle, because that would be more than a penny, only I haven't got to pay for it."

"It must be sweeties!" said Miss Muggins.

"No," said Milly-Molly-Mandy, "but I'll remember soon. Good morning, Miss Muggins!"

So Milly-Molly-Mandy went on to Mr Blunt's, and gave him Uncle's message, and then she sat down on the doorstep and thought and thought what that penny could be for.

And she couldn't remember.

But she remembered one thing: "It's for Aunty," she thought, "and I love Aunty." And she thought for just a little while longer. Then suddenly she sprang up and went back to Miss Muggins' shop.

"I've remembered!" she said. "It's needles for Aunty!"

So Miss Muggins put the packet of needles into the basket, and took the penny, and Milly-Molly-Mandy set off for home.

"That's a good little messenger to remember all those things!" said Mother, when she got there. They were just going to begin dinner. "I thought you were only going with my eggs!"

"She went for my trowel!" said Father.

"And my string!" said Grandpa.

"And my wool!" said Grandma.

"And my chicken-feed!" said Uncle.

"And my needles!" said Aunty.

Then they all laughed; and Grandpa, feeling in his pocket, said:

"Well, here's another errand for you – go and get yourself some sweeties!"

So after dinner Toby had a nice walk and his mistress got her sweets. And then Milly-Molly-Mandy and little-friend-Susan had a lovely time on the see-saw, chatting and eating raspberry-drops, and feeling very happy and contented indeed.

Milly-Molly-Mandy Goes Gardening

ONCE UPON A TIME, one Saturday morning, Milly-Molly-Mandy went down to the village. She had to go to Mr Blunt's corn-shop to order a list of things for Uncle – and would Mr Blunt please send them on Monday without fail?

Mr Blunt said, "Surely, surely! Tell your uncle he shall have them first thing in the morning."

And then Milly-Molly-Mandy, who loved the smell of the corn-shop, peeped into the great bins, and dug her hands down into the maize and bran and oats and let them sift through her fingers. And then she said good-bye and came out.

As she passed the Blunts' little garden at the side of the shop she saw Billy Blunt's back, bending down just the other side of the palings. It looked very busy.

Billy Blunt was a little bigger than Milly-Molly-Mandy, and she did not know him very well, but they always said "Hullo!" when they met.

So Milly-Molly-Mandy peeped through the palings and said, "Hullo, Billy!"

Billy Blunt looked round for a moment and said, "Hullo!" And then he turned back to his work.

But he didn't say, "Hullo, Milly-Molly-Mandy!" and he didn't smile. So Milly-Molly-Mandy stuck her toes in the fence and hung on and looked over the top.

"What's the matter?" Milly-Molly-Mandy asked.

Billy Blunt looked round again. "Nothing's the matter," he said gloomily. "Only I've got to weed these old flower-beds right up to the house."

"I don't mind weeding," said Milly-Molly-Mandy.

"Huh! You try it here, and see how you like it!" said Billy Blunt.

"The earth's as hard as nails, and the weeds have got roots pretty near a mile long."

Milly-Molly-Mandy wasn't quite sure whether he meant it as an invitation, but anyhow she accepted it as one, and pushed open the little white gate and came into the Blunts' garden.

It was a nice garden, smelling of wallflowers.

Billy Blunt said, "There's a garden-fork." So Milly-Molly-Mandy took it up and started work on the other side of the flower-bed which bordered the little brick path up to the house. And they dug away together.

Presently Milly-Molly-Mandy said, "Doesn't the earth smell nice when you turn it up?"

And Billy Blunt said, "Does it? Yes, it does rather." And they went on weeding.

Presently Milly-Molly-Mandy, pulling tufts of grass out of the pansies, asked, "What do you do this for, if you don't like it?"

And Billy Blunt, tugging at a dandelion root, grunted and said, "Father says I ought to be making myself useful."

"That's our sort of fruit," said Milly-Molly-Mandy. "My Muvver says we'd be like apple-trees which didn't grow apples if we didn't be useful."

"Huh!" said Billy Blunt. "Funny idea, us growing fruit! Never thought of it like that." And they went on weeding.

Presently Milly-Molly-Mandy asked, "Why're there all those little holes in the lawn?"

"Dad's been digging out dandelions," said Billy Blunt. "He wants to make the garden nice."

Then Milly-Molly-Mandy said, "There's lots of grass here, only it oughtn't to be. We might plant it in the holes."

"Umm!" said Billy Blunt. "And then we'll be making the lawn look as tidy as the beds. Let's!"

So they dug, and they turned the earth, and they pulled out what didn't belong there. And all the weeds they threw into a heap to be burned, and all the tufts of grass they carefully planted in the lawn. And after a time the flower-beds began to look most beautifully neat, and you could see hardly any bald places on the lawn.

Presently Mr Blunt came out of the shop on to the pavement. He had a can of green paint and a brush in his hand, and he reached over the palings and set them down among the daisies on the lawn.

"Hullo, Milly-Molly-Mandy!" said Mr Blunt. "Thought you'd gone home. Well, you two have been doing good work on those beds there. Billy, I'm going to paint the water-butt and the handle of the roller some time. Perhaps you'd like to do it for me? You'll have to clean off the rust first with sandpaper."

Billy Blunt and Milly-Molly-Mandy looked quite eager.

Billy Blunt said, "Rather, Dad!" And Milly-Molly-Mandy looked with great interest at the green can and the garden-roller. But she knew she ought to be starting back to dinner at the nice white cottage with the thatched roof, or Father and Mother and Grandpa and Grandma and Uncle and Aunty would be wondering what had become of her. So she handed her garden-fork back to Billy Blunt and walked slowly to the gate.

But Billy Blunt said, "Couldn't you come again after dinner? I'll save you some of the painting."

So Milly-Molly-Mandy gave a little skip and said, "I'd like to, if Muvver doesn't want me."

So after dinner, when she had helped with the washing-up, Milly-Molly-Mandy ran hoppity-skip all the way down to the village again. And there in the Blunts' garden was Billy Blunt, busy rubbing the iron bands on the water-butt with a sheet of sandpaper.

"Hullo, Billy!" said Milly-Molly-Mandy.

"Hullo, Milly-Molly-Mandy!" said Billy Blunt. He looked very hot and dirty, but he smiled quite broadly. And then he said, "I've saved the garden-roller for you to paint – it's all sandpapered ready."

Milly-Molly-Mandy thought that was nice of Billy Blunt, for the sandpapering was the nasty, dirty part of the work.

Billy Blunt got the lid off the can, and stirred up the beautiful green paint with a stick. Then all by himself he thought of fetching a piece of newspaper to pin over her frock to keep her clean.

And then he went back to rubbing the water-butt, while Milly-Molly-Mandy dipped the brush carefully into the lovely full can of green paint, and started work on the garden-roller.

The handle had a pattern in wriggly bits of iron, and it was great fun getting the paint into all the cracks. And you can't imagine how beautiful and new that roller looked when the paint was on it.

Billy Blunt had to keep leaving his water-butt to see how it was going on, because the wriggly bits looked so nice when they were green, and he hadn't any wriggly bits on his water-butt.

By the end of the afternoon you ought to have seen how nice the garden looked! The flower-beds were clean and trim, the lawn tidied up, the water-butt stood glistening green by the side of the house, and the roller lay glistening green on the grass.

And when Mr Blunt came out and saw it all he was pleased!

He called Mrs Blunt, and Mrs Blunt was pleased too. She gave them each a banana, and they ate them sitting on one of the corn-bins in the shop.

And afterwards Billy Blunt buried Milly-Molly-Mandy in the corn, right up to the neck. And when he helped her out again she was all bits of corn, down her neck, and in her socks, and on her hair. But Milly-Molly-Mandy didn't mind a scrap. She liked it.

Milly-Molly-Mandy Keeps Shop

ONCE UPON A TIME Milly-Molly-Mandy was walking home from school with some little friends – Billy Blunt, Miss Muggins' niece Jilly, and, of course, little-friend-Susan. And they were all talking about what they would like to do when they were big.

Billy Blunt said he would have a motor-bus and drive people to the station and pull their boxes about. Miss Muggins' Jilly said she would curl her hair and be a lady who acts for the pictures. Little-friend-Susan wanted to be a nurse with long white streamers, and push a pram with two babies in it.

Milly-Molly-Mandy wanted a shop like Miss Muggins', where she could sell sweets, and cut pretty coloured stuff for people's dresses with a big pair of scissors. And, "Oh, dear!" said Milly-Molly-Mandy. "I wish we didn't have to wait till we had growed up!"

Then they came to Miss Muggins' shop, and Jilly said, "Good-bye," and went in.

And then they came to Mr Blunt's corn-shop, which was only a few steps farther on, and Billy Blunt said, "Good-bye," and went in.

And then Milly-Molly-Mandy and little-friend-Susan, with their arms round each other, walked up the white road with the fields each side till they came to the Moggs' cottage, and little-friend-Susan said, "Good-bye," and went in.

And Milly-Molly-Mandy went hoppity-skipping on alone till she came to the nice white cottage with the thatched roof, where Mother was at the gate to meet her.

Next day was Saturday, and Milly-Molly-Mandy went down to the village on an errand for Mother. And when she had done it she saw Miss Muggins standing at her shop door, looking rather worried.

And when Miss Muggins saw Milly-Molly-Mandy she said, "Oh, Milly-Molly-Mandy, would you mind running to ask Mrs Jakes if she could come and mind my shop for an hour? Tell her I've got to go to see someone on very important business, and I don't know what to do, and Jilly's gone picnicking."

So Milly-Molly-Mandy ran to ask Mrs Jakes. But Mrs Jakes said, "Tell Miss Muggins I'm very sorry, but I've just got the cakes in the oven, and I can't leave them."

So Milly-Molly-Mandy ran back and told Miss Muggins, and Miss Muggins said, "I wonder if Mrs Blunt would come."

So Milly-Molly-Mandy ran to ask Mrs Blunt. But Mrs Blunt said, "I'm sorry, but I'm simply up to my eyes in house-cleaning, and I can't leave just now."

So Milly-Molly-Mandy ran back and told Miss Muggins, and Miss Muggins said she didn't know of anyone else she could ask.

Then Milly-Molly-Mandy said, "Oh, Miss Muggins, couldn't I look after the shop for you? I'll tell people you'll be back in an hour, and if they only want a sugar-stick or something I could give it them – I know how much it is!"

Miss Muggins looked at Milly-Molly-Mandy, and then she said, "Well, you aren't very big, but I know you're careful, Milly-Molly-Mandy."

So she gave her lots of instructions about asking people if they would come back in an hour, and not selling things unless she was quite sure of the price, and so on. And then Miss Muggins put on her hat and feather boa and hurried off.

And Milly-Molly-Mandy was left alone in charge of the shop!

Milly-Molly-Mandy felt very solemn and careful indeed. She dusted the counter with a duster which she saw hanging on a nail; and then she peeped into the window at all the handkerchiefs and socks and bottles of sweets – and she could see Mrs Hubble arranging the loaves and cakes in her shop-window opposite, and Mr Smale (who had the grocer's shop with a little counter at the back where you posted parcels and bought stamps and letter-paper) standing at his door enjoying the sunshine. And Milly-Molly-Mandy felt so pleased that she had a shop as well as they.

And then, suddenly, the door-handle rattled, and the little bell over the door jangle-jangled up and down, and who should come in but little-friend-Susan!

And how little-friend-Susan did stare when she saw Milly-Molly-Mandy behind the counter!

"Miss Muggins has gone out on 'portant business, but she'll be back in an hour. What do you want?" said Milly-Molly-Mandy.

"A packet of safety-pins for Mother. What are you doing here?" said little-friend-Susan.

"I'm looking after the shop," said Milly-Molly-Mandy. "And I know where the safety-pins are, because I had to buy some yesterday."

So Milly-Molly-Mandy wrapped up the safety-pins in a piece of thin brown paper, and twisted the end just as Miss Muggins did. And she handed the packet to little-friend-Susan, and little-friend-Susan handed her a penny.

And then little-friend-Susan wanted to stay and play "shops" with Milly-Molly-Mandy.

But Milly-Molly-Mandy shook her head solemnly and said, "No, this isn't play; it's business. I've got to be very, very careful. You'd better go, Susan."

And just then the bell jangled again, and a lady came in, so little-friend-Susan went out. (She peered through the window for a time to see how Milly-Molly-Mandy got on, but Milly-Molly-Mandy wouldn't look at her.)

The lady was Miss Bloss, who lived opposite, over the baker's shop, with Mrs Bloss. She wanted a quarter of a yard of pink flannelette, because she was making a wrapper for her mother, and she hadn't bought quite enough for the collar. She said she didn't like to waste a whole hour till Miss Muggins returned.

Milly-Molly-Mandy stood on one leg and wondered what to do, and Miss Bloss tapped with one finger and wondered what to do.

And then Miss Bloss said, "That's the roll my flannelette came off. I'm quite sure Miss Muggins wouldn't mind my taking some."

So between them they measured off the pink flannelette, and Milly-Molly-Mandy fetched Miss Muggins' big scissors, and Miss Bloss made a crease exactly where the quarter-yard came; and Milly-Molly-Mandy breathed very hard and cut slowly and carefully right along the crease to the end.

And then she wrapped the piece up and gave it to Miss Bloss, and Miss Bloss handed her half a crown, saying, "Ask Miss Muggins to send me the change when she gets back."

And then Miss Bloss went out.

And then for a time nobody came in, and Milly-Molly-Mandy amused herself by trying to find the rolls of stuff that different people's dresses had come off. There was her own pink-and-white-striped cotton (looking so lovely and new) and Mother's blue-checked apron stuff and Mrs Jakes' Sunday gown . . .

Then rattle went the handle and jangle went the bell, and who should come in but Billy Blunt!

"I'm Miss Muggins," said Milly-Molly-Mandy. "What do you want to buy?"

"Where's Miss Muggins?" said Billy Blunt.

So Milly-Molly-Mandy had to explain again. And then Billy Blunt said he had wanted a pennyworth of aniseed-balls. So Milly-Molly-Mandy stood on a box and reached down the glass jar from the shelf.

They were twelve a penny she knew, for she had often bought them. So she counted them out, and then Billy Blunt counted them.

And Billy Blunt said, "You've got one too many here."

So Milly-Molly-Mandy counted again, and she found one too many too. So they dropped one back in the jar, and Milly-Molly-Mandy put the others into a little bag and swung it over by the corners, just as Miss Muggins did, and gave it to Billy Blunt. And Billy Blunt gave her his penny.

And then Billy Blunt grinned, and said, "Good morning, ma'am."

And Milly-Molly-Mandy said, "Good morning, sir," and Billy Blunt went out.

After that an hour began to seem rather a long time, with the sun shining so outside. But at last the little bell gave a lively jangle again, and Miss Muggins had returned!

And though Milly-Molly-Mandy had enjoyed herself very much, she thought perhaps, after all, she would rather wait until she was grown up before she kept a shop for herself.

Milly-Molly-Mandy Goes to a Party

ONCE UPON A TIME something very nice happened in the village where Milly-Molly-Mandy and her Father and Mother and Grandpa and Grandma and Uncle and Aunty lived. Some ladies clubbed together to give a party to all the children in the village, and of course Milly-Molly-Mandy was invited.

Little-friend-Susan had an invitation too, and Billy Blunt (whose father kept the corn-shop where Milly-Molly-Mandy's Uncle got his chicken-feed), and Jilly, the little niece of Miss Muggins (who kept the shop where Milly-Molly-Mandy's Grandma bought her knitting-wool), and lots of others whom Milly-Molly-Mandy knew.

It *was* exciting.

Milly-Molly-Mandy had not been to a real party for a long time, so she was very pleased and interested when Mother said, "Well, Milly-Molly-Mandy, you must have a proper new dress for a party like this. We must think what we can do."

So Mother and Grandma and Aunty thought together for a bit, and then Mother went to the big wardrobe and rummaged in her bottom drawer until she found a most beautiful white silk scarf, which she had worn when she was married to Father, and it was just wide enough to be made into a party frock for Milly-Molly-Mandy.

Then Grandma brought out of her best handkerchief-box a most beautiful lace handkerchief, which would just cut into a little collar for the neck of the party frock.

And Aunty brought out of her small top drawer some most beautiful pink ribbon, all smelling of lavender – just enough to make into a sash for the party frock.

And then Mother and Aunty set to work to cut and stitch at the party frock, while Milly-Molly-Mandy jumped up and down and handed pins when they were wanted.

The next day Father came in with a paper parcel for Milly-Molly-Mandy bulging in his coat-pocket, and when Milly-Molly-Mandy unwrapped it she found the most beautiful little pair of red shoes inside!

And then Grandpa came in and held out his closed hand to Milly-Molly-Mandy, and when Milly-Molly-Mandy got his fingers open she found the most beautiful little coral necklace inside!

And then Uncle came in, and he said to Milly-Molly-Mandy, "What have I done with my handkerchief?" And he felt in all his pockets. "Oh, here it is!" And he pulled out the most beautiful little handkerchief with a pink border, which of course Milly-Molly-Mandy just knew was meant for her, and she wouldn't let Uncle wipe his nose on it, which he pretended he was going to do!

Milly-Molly-Mandy was so pleased she hugged everybody in turn – Father, Mother, Grandpa, Grandma, Uncle, and Aunty.

At last the great day arrived, and little-friend-Susan, in her best spotted dress and silver bangle, called for Milly-Molly-Mandy, and they went together to the village institute, where the party was to be.

There was a lady outside who welcomed them in, and there were more ladies inside who helped them take their things off. And everywhere looked so pretty, with garlands of coloured paper looped from the ceiling, and everybody in their best clothes.

Most of the boys and girls were looking at a row of toys on the mantelpiece, and a lady explained that they were all prizes, to be won by the children who got the most marks in the games they were going to have. There was a lovely fairy doll and a big teddy bear and a picture-book and all sorts of things.

And at the end of the row was a funny little white cotton-wool rabbit with a pointed paper hat on his head. And directly Milly-Molly-Mandy saw him she wanted him dreadfully badly, more than any of the other things.

Little-friend-Susan wanted the picture-book, and Miss Muggins' niece, Jilly, wanted the fairy doll. But the black, beady eyes of the little cotton-wool rabbit gazed so wistfully at Milly-Molly-Mandy that she determined to try ever so hard in all the games and see if she could win him.

Then the games began, and they *were* fun! They had a spoon-and-potato race, and musical chairs, and putting the tail on the donkey blindfold, and all sorts of guessing games.

And then they had supper – bread-and-butter with coloured hundreds-and-thousands sprinkled on, and red jellies and yellow jellies, and cakes with icing and cakes with cherries, and lemonade in red glasses.

It was quite a proper party.

And at the end the names of prize-winners were called out, and the children had to go up and receive their prizes.

And what do you think Milly-Molly-Mandy got?

Why, she had tried so hard to win the little cotton-wool rabbit that she won first prize instead, and got the lovely fairy doll!

And Miss Muggins' niece Jilly, who hadn't won any of the games, got the little cotton-wool rabbit with the sad, beady eyes – for do you know, the cotton-wool rabbit was only the booby prize, after all!

It was a lovely fairy doll, but Milly-Molly-Mandy was sure Miss Muggins' Jilly wasn't loving the booby rabbit as it ought to be loved, for its beady eyes did look so sad, and when she got near Miss Muggins' Jilly she stroked the booby rabbit, and Miss Muggins' Jilly stroked the fairy doll's hair.

Then Milly-Molly-Mandy said, "Do you love the fairy doll more than the booby rabbit?"

And Miss Muggins' Jilly said, "I should think so!"

So Milly-Molly-Mandy ran up to the lady who had given the prizes, and asked if she and Miss Muggins' Jilly might exchange prizes, and the lady said, "Yes, of course."

So Milly-Molly-Mandy and the booby rabbit went home together to the nice white cottage with the thatched roof, and Father and Mother and Grandpa and Grandma and Uncle and Aunty all liked the booby rabbit very much indeed.

And do you know, one day one of his little bead eyes dropped off, and when Mother had stuck it on again with a dab of glue, his eyes didn't look a bit sad any more, but almost as happy as Milly-Molly-Mandy's own!

Milly-Molly-Mandy Goes to the Sea

ONCE UPON A TIME – what *do* you think? – Milly-Molly-Mandy was going to be taken to the seaside!

Milly-Molly-Mandy had never seen the sea in all her life before, and ever since Mother came back from her seaside holiday with her friend Mrs Hooker, and told Milly-Molly-Mandy about the splashy waves and the sand and the little crabs, Milly-Molly-Mandy had just longed to go there herself.

Father and Mother and Grandpa and Grandma and Uncle and Aunty just longed for her to go too, because they knew she would like it so much. But they were all so busy, and then, you know, holidays cost quite a lot of money.

So Milly-Molly-Mandy played "seaside" instead, by the little brook in the meadow, with little-friend-Susan and Billy Blunt and the shells Mother had brought home for her. (And it was a very nice game indeed, but still Milly-Molly-Mandy did wish sometimes that it could be the real sea!)

Then one day little-friend-Susan went with her mother and baby sister to stay with a relation who let lodgings by the sea. And little-friend-Susan wrote Milly-Molly-Mandy a postcard saying how lovely it was, and how she did wish Milly-Molly-Mandy was there; and Mrs Moggs wrote Mother a postcard saying couldn't some of them manage to come down just for a day excursion, one Saturday?

Father and Mother and Grandpa and Grandma and Uncle and Aunty thought something really ought to be done about that, and they talked it over, while Milly-Molly-Mandy listened with all her ears.

But Father said he couldn't go, because he had to get his potatoes up; Mother said she couldn't go, because it was baking day, and, besides, she had just had a lovely seaside holiday; Grandpa said he couldn't go, because it was market-day; Grandma said she wasn't really very fond of train journeys; Uncle said he oughtn't to leave his cows and chickens.

But then they all said Aunty could quite well leave the sweeping and dusting for that one day.

So Aunty only said it seemed too bad that she should have all the fun. And then she and Milly-Molly-Mandy hugged each other, because it was so very exciting.

Milly-Molly-Mandy ran off to tell Billy Blunt at once, because she felt she would burst if she didn't tell someone. And Billy Blunt did wish he could be going too, but his father and mother were always busy.

Milly-Molly-Mandy told Aunty, and Aunty said, "Tell Billy Blunt to ask his mother to let him come with us, and I'll see after him!"

So Billy Blunt did, and Mrs Blunt said it was very kind of Aunty and she'd be glad to let him go.

Milly-Molly-Mandy hoppity-skipped like anything, because she was so very pleased; and Billy Blunt was very pleased too, though he didn't hoppity-skip, because he always thought he was too old for such doings (but he wasn't really!).

So now they were able to plan together for Saturday, which made it much more fun.

Mother had an old bathing-dress which she cut down to fit Milly-Molly-Mandy, and the bits over she made into a flower for the shoulder (and it looked a very smart bathing-dress indeed). Billy Blunt borrowed a swimming-suit from another boy at school (but it hadn't any flower on the shoulder, of course not!).

Then Billy Blunt said to Milly-Molly-Mandy, "If you've got swimming-suits you ought to swim. We'd better practise."

But Milly-Molly-Mandy said, "We haven't got enough water."

Billy Blunt said, "Practise in air, then – better than nothing."

So they fetched two old boxes from the barn out into the yard, and then lay on them (on their fronts) and spread out their arms and kicked with their legs just as if they were swimming.

And when Uncle came along to fetch a wheelbarrow he said it really made him feel quite cool to see them! He showed them how to turn their hands properly, and kept calling out, "Steady! Steady! Not so fast!" as he watched them. And then Uncle lay on his front on the box and showed them how (and he looked so funny!), and then they tried again, and Uncle said it was better that time.

So they practised until they were quite out of breath. And then they pretended to dive off the boxes, and they splashed and swallowed mouthfuls of air and swam races to the gate and shivered and dried themselves with old sacks – and it was almost as much fun as if it were real water!

Well, Saturday came at last, and Aunty and Milly-Molly-Mandy met Billy Blunt at nine o'clock by the cross-roads. And then they went in the red bus to the station in the next town. And then they went in the train, *rumpty-te-tump*, *rumpty-te-tump*, all the way down to the sea.

And you can't imagine how exciting it was, when they got out at last, to walk down a road knowing they would see the real sea at the bottom! Milly-Molly-Mandy got so excited that she didn't want to look till they were up quite close.

So Billy Blunt (who had seen it once before) pulled her along right on to the edge of the sand, and then he said suddenly, "Now look!"

And Milly-Molly-Mandy looked.

And there was the sea, all jumping with sparkles in the sunshine, as far as ever you could see. And little-friend-Susan, with bare legs and frock tucked up, came tearing over the sand to meet them from where Mrs Moggs and Baby Moggs were sitting by a wooden breakwater.

Wasn't it fun!

They took off their shoes and their socks and their hats, and they wanted to take off their clothes and bathe, but Aunty said they must have dinner first. So they sat round and ate sandwiches and cake and fruit which Aunty had brought in a basket. And the Moggses had theirs too out of a basket.

Then they played in the sand with Baby Moggs (who liked having her legs buried), and paddled a bit and found crabs (they didn't take them away from the water, though).

And then Aunty and Mrs Moggs said they might bathe now if they wanted to. So (as it was a very quiet sort of beach) Milly-Molly-Mandy undressed behind Aunty, and little-friend-Susan undressed behind Mrs Moggs, and Billy Blunt undressed behind the breakwater.

And then they ran right into the water in their bathing-dresses. (And little-friend-Susan thought Milly-Molly-Mandy's bathing-dress *was* smart, with the flower on the shoulder!)

But, dear me! water-swimming feels so different from land-swimming, and Milly-Molly-Mandy couldn't manage at all well with the little waves splashing at her all the time. Billy Blunt swished about in the water with a very grim face, and looked exactly as if he were swimming; but when Milly-Molly-Mandy asked him, he said, "No! My arms swim, but my legs only walk!"

It was queer, for it had seemed quite easy in the barnyard.

But they went on pretending and pretending to swim until Aunty called them out. And then they dried themselves with towels and got into their clothes again; and Billy Blunt said, well, anyhow, he supposed they were just that much nearer swimming properly than they were before; and Milly-Molly-Mandy said she supposed next time they might p'r'aps be able to lift their feet off the ground for a minute at any rate; and little-friend-Susan said she was sure she had swallowed a shrimp! (But that was only her fun!)

Then they played and explored among the rock-pools and had tea on the sand. And after tea Mrs Moggs and Baby Moggs and little-friend-Susan walked with them back to the station; and Aunty and Milly-Molly-Mandy and Billy Blunt went in the train, *rumpty-te-tump*, *rumpty-te-tump*, all the way home again.

And Milly-Molly-Mandy was so sleepy when she got to the nice white cottage with the thatched roof that she had only just time to kiss Father and Mother and Grandpa and Grandma and Uncle and Aunty good-night and get into bed before she fell fast asleep.

But she did have a lot to talk about next day!

Milly-Molly-Mandy Dresses Up

ONCE UPON A TIME Milly-Molly-Mandy found an old skirt. She and little-friend-Susan were playing up in the attic of the nice white cottage with the thatched roof (where Milly-Molly-Mandy lived). They had turned out the rag-bags and dressed themselves in all sorts of things – blouses with the sleeves cut off, worn-out curtains, old night-gowns and shirts, and some of Milly-Molly-Mandy's own out-grown frocks (which Mother kept for patching her present ones, when needed).

Milly-Molly-Mandy and little-friend-Susan looked awfully funny – especially when they tried to put on the things which Milly-Molly-Mandy had outgrown. They laughed and laughed.

(The attic was rather a nice place for laughing in – it sort of echoed.)

Well, when Milly-Molly-Mandy found the old skirt of Mother's, of course she put it on. The waist had to fasten round her chest to make it short enough, but that didn't matter. She put on over it an old jumper

43

with a burnt place in front, but she wore it back to front; so that didn't matter either.

Milly-Molly-Mandy walked up and down the attic, feeling just like Mother. She even wore a little brass curtain-ring on the finger of her left hand like Mother.

And then she had an idea.

"Let's both dress up and be ladies," said Milly-Molly-Mandy.

"Ooh, yes, let's," said little-friend-Susan.

So they picked out things from the rag-bags as best they could, and little-friend-Susan put on a dress which was quite good in front, only it had no back. She pulled her curls up on to the top of her head and tied them there with a bit of ribbon.

Milly-Molly-Mandy tucked her hair behind her ears and fastened it behind with a bit of string, so that it made a funny sort of bun.

"We ought to wear coats and hats," said Milly-Molly-Mandy, "then we'd look quite all right."

So they went downstairs in their long skirts, and Milly-Molly-Mandy took Aunty's mackintosh from the pegs by the kitchen door for little-friend-Susan, and she borrowed an old jacket of Mother's for herself. They borrowed their hats too (not their best ones, of course), and went up to Mother's room to look in the mirror. They trimmed themselves up a bit from the rag-bags, and admired each other, and strutted about, enjoying themselves like anything.

And just then Mother called up the stairs:

"Milly-Molly-Mandy?"

"Yes, Mother?" Milly-Molly-Mandy called down the stairs.

"When you go out, Milly-Molly-Mandy, please go to the Grocer's and get me a tin of treacle. I shall be wanting some for making gingerbread. I've put the money on the bottom stair here."

So Milly-Molly-Mandy said: "Yes, Mother. I'll just go, Mother."

And then Milly-Molly-Mandy looked at little-friend-Susan. And little-friend-Susan looked at Milly-Molly-Mandy. And they said to each other, both at the same time:

"DARE you to go and get it like this!"

"Ooh!" said Milly-Molly-Mandy; and "Ooh!" said little-friend-Susan. "*Dare* we?"

"I'd have to tuck up my sleeves – they're too long," said Milly-Molly-Mandy. "Tell you what, Susan, we might go by the fields instead of down the road; then we wouldn't meet so many people. Look, I'll carry a shopping-basket, and you can take an umbrella, because it's easier when you've got something to carry. Come on."

So Milly-Molly-Mandy and little-friend-Susan crept downstairs and out at the front door, so that Father and Mother and Grandpa and Grandma and Uncle and Aunty mightn't see them. And they went down the front path to the gate.

But there was a horse and cart clip-clopping along the road, so they hung back and waited till it went by. And what do you think? The man driving it saw someone's back-view behind the gate, and he must have taken for granted it was Mother or Aunty or Grandma, for he called out, "Morning, ma'am!" as he passed.

Milly-Molly-Mandy and little-friend-Susan were so pleased they laughed till they had to hold each other up. But it made them feel much better.

They straightened their hats and hitched their skirts, and then they opened the gate and walked boldly across the road to the stile in the hedge on the other side.

It was quite a business getting over that stile. Milly-Molly-Mandy and little-friend-Susan had to rearrange themselves carefully again on the other side.

Then, with their basket and umbrella, the two ladies set off along the narrow path across the field.

"Now, we mustn't laugh," said Milly-Molly-Mandy. "Ladies don't laugh a lot, not outdoors. We shall give ourselves away if we keep laughing."

"No," said little-friend-Susan, "we mustn't. But suppose we meet Billy Blunt?"

"We mustn't run, either," said Milly-Molly-Mandy. "Ladies don't run much."

"No," said little-friend-Susan, "we mustn't. But I do hope we don't meet Billy Blunt."

"So do I," said Milly-Molly-Mandy. "I'd like to meet him worst of anybody. He'd be sure to know us. We mustn't keep looking round, either, Susan. Ladies don't keep on looking round."

"I was only wondering if anyone could see us," said little-friend-Susan.

But there were only cows on the far side of the meadow, and they weren't at all interested in the two rather short ladies walking along the narrow path.

Soon Milly-Molly-Mandy and little-friend-Susan came to the stile into Church Lane. This was a rather high stile, and while she was getting over it the band of Milly-Molly-Mandy's skirt slipped from her chest to her waist, and her feet got tangled in the length of it. She came down on all fours into the grass at the side, with her hat over one eye. But, luckily, she just got straightened up before they saw the old gardener-man who looked after the churchyard coming along up the lane with his wheel-barrow.

"Let's wait till he's gone," said Milly-Molly-Mandy. "We'll be looking in my basket, so we needn't look up."

So they rummaged in the basket (which held only a bit of paper with the money in it), and talked in ladylike tones, until the old gardener-man had passed by.

He stared rather, and looked back at them once, but the two ladies were too busy to notice him.

When he was safely through the churchyard gate they went down the lane till they came to the forge at the bottom.

Mr Rudge the Blacksmith was banging away on his anvil. He was a nice man, and Milly-Molly-Mandy and little-friend-Susan thought it would be fun to stop and see what he thought of them. So they stood at the doorway and watched him hammering at a piece of red-hot iron he was holding with his tongs.

Mr Rudge glanced up at them. And then he looked down. And then he went on hammering. And then he turned and put the piece of iron into the furnace. And while he worked the handle of the big bellows slowly up and down (to make the fire burn hot) he looked at them again over his shoulder, and said:

"Good morning, ladies. It's a warm day today."

"Yes, it is," agreed Milly-Molly-Mandy and little-friend-Susan. (They were feeling very warm indeed, though it wasn't at all sunny out.)

"Visitors in these parts, I take it," said the Blacksmith.

"Yes, we are," agreed Milly-Molly-Mandy and little-friend-Susan.

Then Milly-Molly-Mandy said: "Can you tell us if there is a good grocer's shop anywhere round here?"

"Let me see, now," said the Blacksmith, thinking hard. "Yes, I believe there is. Try going to the end of this lane, here, and turn sharp right – very sharp, mind. Then look both ways at once, and cross the road. You'll maybe see one."

Then he took his iron out, all red-hot, and began hammering at it again to shape it.

Milly-Molly-Mandy and little-friend-Susan couldn't be quite sure whether Mr Rudge knew them or not. They were just thinking of going on when – *who* should come round the corner of Mr Blunt's corn-shop but Billy Blunt himself!

Billy Blunt noticed the two rather odd-looking ladies standing in front of the forge. And he noticed one of them pull the other's sleeve, which came right down over her hand. And then they both turned and walked up the lane.

He thought they looked a bit queer somehow – short and rather crumpled. So he stopped at the forge and asked the Blacksmith:

"Who are those two?"

"Lady-friends of mine," said the Blacksmith, turning the iron and getting hold of it in a different place. "Lady-friends. Known 'em for years."

Billy Blunt waited, but the Blacksmith didn't say anything more. So he began strolling up the lane after the two ladies, who were near the stile by now.

The lady in the mackintosh seemed to be a bit flustered, whispering to the other. Then the other one said (so that he could hear):

"I seem to have lost my shopping-list, it isn't in my basket. Have you got it, dear?"

Billy Blunt strolled nearer. He wanted to see their faces.

"No, I haven't got it," said the first one. "We'd better go home and look for it. Oh, dear, I think it's coming on to rain. I felt a little spit. I must put up my umbrella."

And she opened it and held it over them both, so that Billy Blunt couldn't see so much of them.

He strolled a bit nearer, and stopped to pick an unripe blackberry from the hedge and put it in his mouth. He wanted to see the ladies climb over the stile.

But they waited there, rummaging in their basket and talking of the rain. Billy Blunt couldn't feel any rain. Presently he heard the lady with the basket say in a rather pointed way:

"I wonder what that *little boy* thinks he's doing there? He ought to go home."

And, quite suddenly, that's what the "little boy" did. At any rate he hurried off down the lane and out of sight.

Then Milly-Molly-Mandy and little-friend-Susan, very relieved, picked up their skirts and scrambled over the stile, and set off back across the fields. There was nobody to see them now but the cows, so they ran, laughing and giggling and tumbling against each other among the buttercups all the way across.

And by the time they got back to the first stile, just opposite the nice white cottage with the thatched roof (where Milly-Molly-Mandy lived), you never saw such a funny-looking pair of ladies!

Little-friend-Susan's hat-trimming had come off, and Milly-Molly-Mandy had stepped right out of her rag-bag skirt after it had tripped her up three times, and they were both so out of breath with giggling that they could hardly climb over on to the road.

But the moment they landed on the other side somebody jumped out at them from the hedge. And WHO do you suppose it was?

Yes, of course! It was Billy Blunt.

He had run all the way round by the road, just for the fun of facing them as they came across that stile.

"Huh! Think I didn't know you?" he asked, breathing hard. "I knew you at once."

"Then why didn't you speak to us?" asked little-friend-Susan.

"Think I'd want to speak to either of you looking like that?" said Billy Blunt, grinning.

"I don't believe you did know us, not just at once," said Milly-Molly-Mandy, "or you'd have said something, even if it was rude!"

"Look!" said little-friend-Susan. "There's someone coming. Let's go in quick!"

So they scurried across the road and through the garden gate. And just then Milly-Molly-Mandy's mother came out to pick a handful of flowers for the table.

"Well, goodness me!" said Mother. "Whatever's all this?"

"We were just dressing up," said Milly-Molly-Mandy, "when you wanted us to go to the village—"

"And we dared each other to go like this—" said little-friend-Susan.

"I saw the two guys talking to the Blacksmith—" said Billy Blunt.

"Anyhow," said Milly-Molly-Mandy, hopping on each leg in turn, her rag-bag hat-trimming looping over one eye, "we did dare, didn't we, Susan?"

"Well, well!" said Mother. "And where's my tin of treacle?"

Milly-Molly-Mandy stopped.

"We forgot all about it! I'm sorry, Mother. We'll go now!"

"Not like that!" said Mother. "You take my coat off, and go in and tidy yourselves first. And the attic, too."

"I'll run and get the treacle for you," said Billy Blunt. "'Spect I stopped 'em – they'd got almost as far as the Grocer's, anyhow."

"Yes, he scared us!" said Milly-Molly-Mandy, handing him Mother's money out of the basket. "He followed us along and never said a word. He thought we were proper ladies, that's why!"

"Thought you were proper guys," said Billy Blunt, going out of the gate.

Milly-Molly-Mandy Gets to Know Teacher

ONCE UPON A TIME there were changes at Milly-Molly-Mandy's school. Miss Sheppard, the head-mistress, was going away, and Miss Edwards, the second teacher, was to be head-mistress in her place, and live in the teacher's cottage just by the school, instead of coming in by the bus from the next town each day.

Miss Edwards was very strict, and taught arithmetic and history and geography, and wore high collars.

Milly-Molly-Mandy wasn't particularly interested in the change, though she liked both Miss Sheppard and Miss Edwards quite well. But one afternoon Miss Edwards gave her a note to give to her Mother, and the note was to ask if Milly-Molly-Mandy's Mother would be so very good as to let Miss Edwards have a bed at the nice white cottage with the thatched roof for a night or two until Miss Edwards got her new little house straight.

Father and Mother and Grandpa and Grandma and Uncle and Aunty talked it over during supper, and they thought they might manage it for a few nights. Milly-Molly-Mandy was very interested, and tried to think what it would be like to have Teacher sitting at supper with them, and going to sleep in the spare room, as well as teaching in school all day. And she couldn't help feeling just a little bit glad that it was only to be for a night or two.

Next day she took a note to school for Teacher from Mother to say, yes, they would be pleased to have her. And after school Milly-Molly-Mandy told little-friend-Susan and Billy Blunt about it.

And little-friend-Susan said, "Ooh! Won't you have to behave properly! I'm glad she's not coming to us!"

And Billy Blunt said, "Huh! – hard lines!"

Milly-Molly-Mandy was quite glad Teacher was only coming to stay for a few nights.

Miss Edwards arrived at the nice white cottage with the thatched roof just before supper-time the following evening.

Milly-Molly-Mandy was looking out for her, and directly she heard the gate click she called Mother and ran and opened the front door wide, so that the hall lamp could shine down the path. And Teacher came in out of the dark, just as Mother hurried from the kitchen to welcome her.

Teacher thanked Mother very much for having her, and said she felt so dusty and untidy because she had been putting up shelves in her new little cottage ever since school was over.

So Mother said, "Come right up to your room, Miss Edwards, and Milly-Molly-Mandy will bring you a jug of hot water. And then I expect you'll be glad of some supper straight away!"

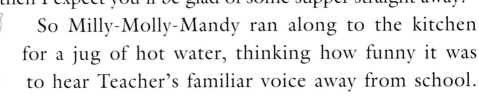

So Milly-Molly-Mandy ran along to the kitchen for a jug of hot water, thinking how funny it was to hear Teacher's familiar voice away from school.

She tapped very politely at the half-open door of the spare room (she could see Teacher tidying her hair in front of the dressing-table, by the candlelight), and Teacher smiled at her as she took the steaming jug, and said:

"That's kind of you, Milly-Molly-Mandy! This is just what I want most. What a lovely smell of hot cakes!"

Milly-Molly-Mandy smiled back, though she was quite a bit surprised that Teacher should speak in that pleased, hungry sort of way – it was more the kind of way she, or little-friend-Susan, or Father or Mother or Grandpa or Grandma or Uncle or Aunty, might have spoken.

When Teacher came downstairs to the kitchen they all sat down to supper. Teacher's place was just opposite Milly-Molly-Mandy's, and every time she caught Milly-Molly-Mandy's eye she smiled across at her. And Milly-Molly-Mandy smiled back, and tried to remember to sit up, for she kept on almost expecting Teacher to say, "Head up, Milly-Molly-Mandy! Keep your elbows off the desk!" – but she never did!

They were all a little shy of Teacher, just at first; but soon Father and Mother and Grandpa and Grandma and Uncle and Aunty were talking away, and Teacher was talking too, and laughing. And she looked so different when she was laughing that Milly-Molly-Mandy found it quite difficult to get on with her bread-and-milk before it got cold. Teacher enjoyed the hot cakes, and wanted to know just how Mother made them. She asked a lot of questions, and Mother said she would teach Teacher how to do it, so that she could make them in her own new little kitchen.

Milly-Molly-Mandy thought how funny it would be for Teacher to start having lessons.

After supper Teacher asked Milly-Molly-Mandy if she could make little sailor-girls, and when Milly-Molly-Mandy said no, Teacher drew a little sailor-girl, with a sailor-collar and sailor-hat and pleated skirt, on a folded piece of paper, and then she cut it out with Aunty's scissors. And when she unfolded the paper there was a whole row of little sailor-girls all holding hands.

Milly-Molly-Mandy did like it. She thought how funny it was that she should have known Teacher all that time and never known she could draw little sailor-girls.

Then Mother said, "Now, Milly-Molly-Mandy, it is bedtime." So Milly-Molly-Mandy kissed Father and Mother and Grandpa and Grandma and Uncle and Aunty, and went to shake hands with Teacher. But Teacher said she wanted a kiss too. So they kissed each other in quite a nice friendly way.

But still Milly-Molly-Mandy felt when she went upstairs she must get into bed extra quickly and quietly, because Teacher was in the house.

Next morning Milly-Molly-Mandy and Teacher went to school together. And as soon as they got there Teacher was just her usual self again, and told Milly-Molly-Mandy to sit up, or to get on with her work, as if she had never laughed at supper, or cut out little sailor-girls, or kissed anyone good-night.

After school Milly-Molly-Mandy showed little-friend-Susan and Billy Blunt the row of little sailor-girls.

And little-friend-Susan opened her eyes and said, "Just fancy Teacher doing that!"

And Billy Blunt folded them up carefully in the creases so that he could see how they were made, and then he grinned and gave them back.

And little-friend-Susan and Billy Blunt didn't feel so very sorry for Milly-Molly-Mandy having Teacher to stay, then.

That evening Teacher came up to the nice white cottage with the thatched roof earlier than she did the day before. And when Milly-Molly-Mandy came into the kitchen from taking a nice meal out to Toby the dog, and giving him a good bedtime romp round the yard, what did she see but Teacher, with one of Mother's big aprons on and her sleeves tucked up, learning how to make apple turn-overs for supper! And Mother was saying, "Always mix pastry with a light hand," and Teacher was looking so interested, and didn't seem in the least to know she had a streak of flour down one cheek.

When Teacher saw Milly-Molly-Mandy she said, "Come along, Milly-Molly-Mandy, and have a cooking lesson with me, it's such fun!"

So Milly-Molly-Mandy's Mother gave her a little piece of dough, and she stood by Teacher's side, rolling it out and making it into a ball again; but she was much more interested in watching Teacher being taught. And Teacher did everything she was told, and tried so hard that her cheeks got quite pink.

When the turn-overs were all made there was a small piece of dough left on the board, so Teacher shaped it into the most beautiful little bird; and the bird and the turn-overs were all popped into the oven, together with Milly-Molly-Mandy's piece (which had been a pig and a cat and a teapot, but ended up a little grey loaf).

When Father and Mother and Grandpa and Grandma and Uncle and Aunty and Teacher and Milly-Molly-Mandy sat down to supper, Teacher put her finger on her lips to Milly-Molly-Mandy when the apple turn-overs came on, so that Milly-Molly-Mandy shouldn't tell who made them until they had been tasted. And Teacher watched anxiously, and presently Mother said, "How do you like these turn-overs?" And everybody said they were most delicious, and then Milly-Molly-Mandy couldn't wait any longer, and she called out, "Teacher made them!" and everybody was so surprised.

Milly-Molly-Mandy didn't eat the little grey-brown loaf, because she didn't quite fancy it (Toby the dog did, though), and she felt she couldn't eat the little golden-brown bird, because it really looked too good to be eaten just yet. So she took it to school with her next day, to share with little-friend-Susan and Billy Blunt.

And little-friend-Susan said, "Isn't it pretty? Isn't Teacher clever?"

And Billy Blunt said, "Fancy Teacher playing with dough!"

And little-friend-Susan and Billy Blunt didn't feel at all sorry for Milly-Molly-Mandy having Teacher to stay, then.

The next day was Saturday, and Teacher's furniture had come, and she was busy all day arranging it and getting the curtains and the pictures up. And Milly-Molly-Mandy with little-friend-Susan and Billy Blunt came in the afternoon to help. And they ran up and down stairs, and fetched hammers and nails, and held things, and made themselves very useful indeed.

And at four o'clock Teacher sent Billy Blunt out to get some cakes from Mrs Hubble's shop, while the others laid the table in the pretty little sitting-room. And they had a nice kind of picnic, with Milly-Molly-Mandy and little-friend-Susan sharing a cup, and Billy Blunt having a saucer for a plate, because everything wasn't unpacked yet. And they all laughed and talked, and were as happy as anything.

And when Teacher said it was time to send them all off home Milly-Molly-Mandy was so sorry to think Teacher wasn't coming to sleep in the spare room any more that she wanted to kiss Teacher without being asked. And she actually did it, too. And little-friend-Susan and Billy Blunt didn't look a bit surprised, either.

And after that, somehow, it didn't seem to matter that Teacher was strict in school, for they knew that she was really just a very nice, usual sort of person inside all the time!

Milly-Molly-Mandy Goes Sledging

ONCE UPON A TIME, one cold grey wintry day, Milly-Molly-Mandy and the others were coming home from school.

It was such a cold wintry day that everybody turned up their coat-collars and put their hands in their pockets, and such a grey wintry day that it seemed almost dark already, though it was only four o'clock.

"Ooh! isn't it a cold grey wintry day!" said Milly-Molly-Mandy.

"Perhaps it's going to snow," said little-friend-Susan.

"Hope it does," said Billy Blunt. "I'm going to make a sledge."

Whereupon Milly-Molly-Mandy and little-friend-Susan said both together: "Ooh! will you give us a ride on it?"

"Haven't made it yet," said Billy Blunt. "But I've got an old wooden box I can make it of."

Then he said good-bye and went in at the side gate by the corn-shop where he lived. And Milly-Molly-Mandy and little-friend-Susan ran together along the road to the Moggs' cottage, where little-friend-Susan lived. And then Milly-Molly-Mandy went on alone to the nice white cottage with the thatched roof, where Toby the dog came capering out to welcome her home.

It felt so nice and warm in the kitchen, and it smelled so nice and warm too, that Milly-Molly-Mandy was quite glad to be in.

"Here she comes!" said Grandma, putting the well-filled toast-rack on the table.

"There you are!" said Aunty, breaking open hot scones and buttering them on a plate.

"Just in time, Milly-Molly-Mandy!" said Mother, pouring boiling water into the teapot. "Call the men-folk in to tea, but don't keep the door open long."

So Milly-Molly-Mandy called, and Father and Grandpa and Uncle soon came in, rubbing their hands, very pleased to get back into the warm again.

"Ah! Nicer indoors than out," said Grandpa.

"There's a feel of snow in the air," said Uncle.

"Shouldn't wonder if we had a fall before morning," said Father.

"Billy Blunt's going to make a sledge, and he *might* let Susan and me have a ride, if it snows," said Milly-Molly-Mandy. And she wished very much that it would. That set Father and Uncle talking during tea of the fun they used to have in their young days sledging down Crocker's Hill.

Milly-Molly-Mandy did wish it would snow soon.

The next day was Saturday, and there was no school, which always made it feel different when you woke up in the morning. But all the same Milly-Molly-Mandy thought something about her little bedroom looked different somehow, when she opened her eyes.

"Milly-Molly-Mandy!" called Mother up the stairs, as she did every morning.

"Yoo-oo!" called Milly-Molly-Mandy, to show she was awake.

"Have you looked out of your window yet?" called Mother.

"No, Mother," called Milly-Molly-Mandy, sitting up in bed. "Why?"

"You look," said Mother. "And hurry up with your dressing." And she went downstairs to the kitchen to get the breakfast.

So Milly-Molly-Mandy jumped out of bed and looked.

"Oh!" she said, staring. "Oh-h!"

For everything outside her little low window was white as white could be, except the sky, which was dark, dirty grey and criss-crossed all over with snowflakes flying down. "Oh-h-h!" said Milly-Molly-Mandy again.

And then she set to work washing and dressing in a great hurry (and wasn't it cold!) and she rushed downstairs.

She wanted to go out and play at once, almost before she had done breakfast, but Mother said there was plenty of time to clear up all her porridge, for she mustn't go out until the snow stopped falling.

Milly-Molly-Mandy hoped it would be quick and stop. She wanted to see little-friend-Susan, and to find out if Billy Blunt had begun making his sledge. But Father said, the deeper the snow the better for sledging. So then Milly-Molly-Mandy didn't know whether she most wished it to snow or to stop snowing!

"Well," said Mother, "it looks as if it means to go on snowing for some while yet, so I should wish for that if I were you! Suppose you be Jemima-Jane and help me to make the cakes this morning, as you can't go out."

So Milly-Molly-Mandy tied on an apron and became Jemima-Jane. And she washed up the breakfast things and put them away; and fetched whatever Mother wanted for cake-making from the larder and the cupboard, and picked over the sultanas (which was a nice job, as Jemima-Jane was allowed to eat as many sultanas as she had fingers on both hands, but not one more), and she beat the eggs in a basin, and stirred the cake-mixture in the bowl. And after Mother had filled the cake tins Jemima-Jane was allowed to put the scrapings into her own little patty-pan and bake it for her own self in the oven (and that sort of cake always tastes nicer than any other sort, only there's never enough of it!)

Well, it snowed and it snowed all day. Milly-Molly-Mandy kept running to the windows to look, but it didn't stop once. When Father and Grandpa and Uncle had to go out (to see after the cows and the pony and the chickens) they came back looking like snowmen.

"Is it good for sledging yet, Father?" asked Milly-Molly-Mandy.

"Getting better every minute, Milly-Molly-Mandy, that's certain," answered Father, stamping snow off his boots on the door-mat.

"I wonder what Susan thinks of it, and if Billy has nearly made his sledge yet," said Milly-Molly-Mandy.

But it didn't stop snowing before dark, so she couldn't find out that day.

The next day, Sunday, the snow had stopped falling, and it looked beautiful, spread out all over everything. Father and Mother and Grandpa and Uncle and Aunty and Milly-Molly-Mandy put on their Wellington boots, or goloshes (Milly-Molly-Mandy had boots), and walked to Church. (Grandma didn't like walking in the snow, so she stayed at home to look after the fire and put the potatoes on.)

Billy Blunt was there with his father and mother, so afterwards in the lane Milly-Molly-Mandy asked him, "Have you made your sledge yet?"

And Billy Blunt said, "'Tisn't finished. Dad's going to help me with it this afternoon. I'll be trying it out before school tomorrow, probably."

Milly-Molly-Mandy was sorry it wasn't done yet. But anyhow she and little-friend-Susan had a grand time all that afternoon, making a snowman in the Moggs' front garden.

On Monday Milly-Molly-Mandy was in a great hurry to finish her breakfast and be off very early to school.

She didn't have long to wait for little-friend-Susan either, and together they trudged along through the snow. It was quite hard going, for sometimes it was almost over the tops of their boots. (But they didn't always keep to the road!)

When they came to the village there, just outside the corn-shop, was Billy Blunt's new sledge. And while they were looking at it Billy Blunt came out at the side gate.

"Hullo," he said. "Thought you weren't coming."

"Hullo, Billy. Isn't that a beauty! Have you been on it yet? Can we have a ride?"

"You'll have to hurry, then," said Billy Blunt, picking up the string. "I've been up on the hill by Crocker's Farm, past the cross-roads."

"I know," said Milly-Molly-Mandy, "near where that little girl Bunchy and her grandmother live. Can we go there now?"

"Hurry up, then," said Billy Blunt.

So they all hurried up, through the village, past the cross-roads and the school, along the road to Crocker's Hill, shuffling through the snow, dragging the sledge behind them.

"Isn't it deep here!" panted Milly-Molly-Mandy. "This is the way Bunchy comes to school every day. I wonder how she'll manage today. She isn't very big."

"We've come uphill a long way," panted little-friend-Susan. "Can't we sit on the sledge and go down now?"

"Oh, let's get to the top of the hill first," panted Milly-Molly-Mandy.

"There's a steep bit there. You get a good run," said Billy Blunt. "I've done it six times. I went up before breakfast."

"I wish I'd come too!" said Milly-Molly-Mandy.

"Sledge only holds one," said Billy Blunt.

"Oh!" said Milly-Molly-Mandy.

"Oh!" said little-friend-Susan.

They hadn't thought of that.

"Which of us has first go?" said little-friend-Susan.

"Don't suppose there'll be time for more than one of you, anyhow," said Billy Blunt. "We've got to get back."

"You have first go," said Milly-Molly-Mandy to little-friend-Susan.

"No, you have first go," said little-friend-Susan to Milly-Molly-Mandy.

"Better hurry," said Billy Blunt. "You'll be late for school."

They struggled on up the last steep bit of the hill.

And there were the little girl Bunchy and her grandmother, hand-in-hand, struggling up it through the snow from the other side. The little cottage where they lived could be seen down below, with their two sets of footprints leading up from it.

"Hullo, Bunchy," said Milly-Molly-Mandy.

"Oh! Hullo, Milly-Molly-Mandy," said Bunchy.

And Bunchy and her grandmother both looked very pleased to see them all. Grandmother had just been thinking she would have to take Bunchy all the way to school today.

But Milly-Molly-Mandy said, "I'll take care of her." And she took hold of Bunchy's little cold hand with her warm one (it was very warm indeed with pulling the sledge up the hill). "You go down in the sledge, Susan, and I'll look after Bunchy."

"No," said little-friend-Susan. "You wanted it just as much."

"Sit *her* on it," said Billy Blunt, pointing to Bunchy. "We can run her to school in no time. Come on."

So Bunchy had the ride, with Billy Blunt to guide the sledge and Milly-Molly-Mandy and little-friend-Susan to keep her safe on it. And Grandmother stood and watched them all go shouting down the steep bit. And then, as Bunchy was quite light and the road was a bit downhill most of the way, they pulled her along easily, right up to the school gate, in good time for school.

And Bunchy *did* enjoy her ride. She thought it was the excitingest thing that had ever happened!

And then after afternoon school (Bunchy had her dinner at school because it was too far for her to go home for it) Billy Blunt told her to get on his sledge again. And he and Milly-Molly-Mandy and little-friend-Susan pulled her all the way home (except up the steepest bit). And Grandmother was so grateful to them that she gave them each a warm currant bun.

And then Milly-Molly-Mandy and little-friend-Susan took turns riding down the hill on Billy Blunt's sledge. It went like the wind, so that you had to shriek like anything, and your cap blew off, and you felt you could go on for ever! And then, *Whoosh!* you landed sprawling in the snow just where the road turned near the bottom.

Milly-Molly-Mandy and little-friend-Susan each got tipped out there. But when Billy Blunt had gone back to the top of the hill with the sledge for his turn he came sailing down and rounded the bend like a bird, and went on and on and was almost at the cross-roads when the others caught him up. (But then, he'd had plenty of practice, and nobody had seen him spill out at his first try!)

It seemed a long walk home to the nice white cottage with the thatched roof after all that, and Milly-Molly-Mandy was quite late for tea. But Father and Mother and Grandpa and Grandma and Uncle and Aunty weren't a bit cross, because they guessed what she had been up to, and of course, you can't go sledging every day!

In fact, it rained that very night, and next day the snow was nearly all gone. So wasn't it a good thing that Billy Blunt had got his sledge made in time?

Milly-Molly-Mandy Goes Carol-Singing

ONCE UPON A TIME Milly-Molly-Mandy heard some funny sounds coming from the little garden at the side of Mr Blunt's corn-shop.

So she looked over the palings, and what should she see but Billy Blunt, looking very solemn and satisfied, blowing away on a big new shiny mouth-organ!

Milly-Molly-Mandy said, "Hullo, Billy!" And Billy Blunt blew "Hullo!" into his mouth-organ (at least, Milly-Molly-Mandy guessed it was that), and went on playing.

Milly-Molly-Mandy waited a bit and listened, and suddenly she found she knew what he was playing.

"It's 'Good King Wenceslas'!" said Milly-Molly-Mandy, "isn't it? Can I have a go soon?"

"I'm practising," said Billy Blunt, stopping for a moment and then going on again.

69

"Practising what?" said Milly-Molly-Mandy.

"Carols," said Billy Blunt.

"What for?" said Milly-Molly-Mandy.

"Don't know," said Billy Blunt, "only it's Christmas-time."

"Then we could go carolling!" said Milly-Molly-Mandy, with a sudden thought. "You could play on your mouth-organ, and I could sing. We could do it outside people's houses on Christmas Eve. Ooh, let's!"

But Billy Blunt only said, "Huh!" and went on blowing his mouth-organ. But he did it rather thoughtfully.

Milly-Molly-Mandy waited a bit longer, and then she was just going to say good-bye when Billy Blunt said, "Here! You can have a go if you want to."

So Milly-Molly-Mandy, very pleased, took the mouth-organ and wiped it on her skirt, and had quite a good "go" (and Billy Blunt knew she was playing "God Save the King"). And then she wiped it again and gave it back, saying, "Good-bye, Billy. Don't forget about the carol-singing," and went on homeward up the white road with the hedges each side.

A few days later (it was the day before Christmas Eve) Billy Blunt came up to the nice white cottage with the thatched roof, where Milly-Molly-Mandy lived, to bring a bag of meal which Uncle had ordered from Mr Blunt's corn-shop for his chickens. Milly-Molly-Mandy was watching Father cut branches of holly from the holly-tree; but when she saw Billy Blunt she thought of the carols, and came running down to the path.

"I say," said Billy Blunt. "About that carol-singing."

"Yes!" said Milly-Molly-Mandy. "Have you been practising hard?"

"Mmm," said Billy Blunt, "I thought we might try 'em over now, if you're still keen on it. Where'll we do it?"

So Milly-Molly-Mandy led the way to the barn; and there in private they made plans and tried over one or two songs. They couldn't do "Hark the Herald Angels Sing" or "Christians Awake", as the top notes in both of them went beyond the top of the mouth-organ, and Billy Blunt wouldn't sing the top notes, because he said it didn't sound proper. But

he could play "Noël" and "While Shepherds Watched" and "Wenceslas" beautifully. So Milly-Molly-Mandy sang while Billy Blunt played, until they could do it together quite nicely.

"I'll have to ask Mother first if I may," said Milly-Molly-Mandy then. So they went round the back way into the kitchen, where Mother and Grandma and Aunty were mixing the Christmas pudding, and Milly-Molly-Mandy asked her question.

Just at first Mother looked a little doubtful. And then she said, "You know Christmas-time is giving time. If you don't mean to knock at the doors and sing for money—"

Milly-Molly-Mandy said, "No, we won't."

"Why, that would be very nice, then," said Mother, "if you do it as nicely as ever you can."

"We'll do it our very best, just for love," said Milly-Molly-Mandy; and Billy Blunt nodded. Then Mother gave them some almonds and bits of peel-sugar, and then Billy Blunt had to go back.

The next day, directly tea was over, Milly-Molly-Mandy, very excited, slipped out of the house in her hat and coat and muffler, and ran down to the gate to look for Billy Blunt.

It was very dark. Presently she saw a bicycle lamp coming along the road. It was jogging up and down in a queer way for a bicycle. And then as it came near it started waving to and fro, and Milly-Molly-Mandy guessed there must be Billy Blunt with it; and she skipped up and down outside the gate, because it did look so exciting and Christmassy!

"You ready? Come on," said Billy Blunt, and the two of them set off down the road.

Soon they came to the Moggs' cottage, and began their carols. At the end of the first song little-friend-Susan's head peered from behind the window curtain, and in the middle of the second she came rushing out of the door, saying, "Oh, wait a bit while I get my hat and coat on, and let me join!"

And Mrs Moggs called from inside, "Susan, bring them in quickly and shut that door, you're chilling the house!"

So they hurried inside and shut the door; and there was Mrs Moggs sitting by the fire with Baby Moggs in her lap, and Mr Moggs was fixing a bunch of holly over the mantelpiece. Mrs Moggs gave them each a lump of toffee, and then Milly-Molly-Mandy and Billy Blunt with little-friend-Susan went off to their carolling.

When they came to the village they meant to sing outside Mr Blunt's corn-shop, and Miss Muggins' draper's shop; but all the little shop-windows were so brightly lit up it made them feel shy.

People were going in and out of Mr Smale the Grocer's shop, and Mrs Hubble the Baker's shop, and sometimes they stopped to look in Miss Muggins' window (which was showing a lot of gay little penny toys and strings of tinsel balls, as well as gloves and handkerchiefs).

Milly-Molly-Mandy said, "Let's wait!" and Billy Blunt said, "Come on!" So they turned into the dark lane by the forge.

They heard the *cling-clang* of a hammer banging on the anvil. And Milly-Molly-Mandy said, "Let's sing to Mr Rudge!" So they went up to the half-open door of the forge.

Billy Blunt blew a little note on the mouth-organ, and they started on their carol.

By the end of the first verse the Blacksmith was bringing his hammer down in time to the music, and it sounded just like a big bell chiming; and then he began joining in, in a big humming sort of voice. And when they finished he shouted out, "Come on in and give us some more!"

So Milly-Molly-Mandy and Billy Blunt and little-friend-Susan came in out of the dark.

It was lovely in the forge, so warm, and full of strange shadows and burnt-leathery sort of smells. They had a warm-up by the fire, and then began another song. And the Blacksmith sang and hammered all to time; and it sounded – as Mr Jakes the Postman popped his head in to say – "real nice and Christmassy!"

"Go on, give us some more," said the Blacksmith, burying his horseshoe in the fire again to make it hot, so that he could punch nail-holes in it.

"We can't do many more," said Milly-Molly-Mandy, "because the mouth-organ isn't quite big enough."

"Oh, never mind that," said the Blacksmith. "Go on, William, give us 'Hark the Herald Angels Sing'!"

So Billy Blunt grinned and struck up, and everybody joined in so lustily that nobody noticed the missing top notes. While they were in the middle of it the door creaked open a little wider, and Miss Muggins' Jilly slipped in to join the fun; and later on Mr and Mrs Blunt strolled over (when they had shut up shop); and then Mr Critch the Thatcher. And soon it seemed as if half the village were in and round the old forge,

singing away, song after song, while the Blacksmith hammered like big bells on his anvil, and got all his horseshoes finished in good time before the holidays.

Presently who should come in but Father! He had been standing outside for quite a time, listening with Mother and Uncle and Aunty and Mr Moggs (they had all strolled down to see what their children were up to, and stopped to join the singing).

But soon Mother beckoned to Milly-Molly-Mandy from behind Father's shoulder, and Miss Muggins peeped round the door and beckoned to Jilly, and Mrs Blunt beckoned to Billy Blunt, and Mr Moggs to little-friend-Susan. They knew that meant bed, but for once they didn't much mind, because it would make Christmas come all the sooner!

So the carols came to an end, and the Blacksmith called out, "What about passing the hat for the carollers?"

But Billy Blunt said with a grin, "You sang, too – louder than we did!"

And little-friend-Susan said, "Everybody sang!"

And Milly-Molly-Mandy said, "We did it for love – all of us!"

And everybody said, "So we did, now!" and wished everybody else "Happy Christmas!"

And then Milly-Molly-Mandy said, "Good-night, see you tomorrow!" to Billy Blunt, and went skipping off home to bed, holding on to Father's hand through the dark.